Here Come the Creatures!

Poems by

WES MAGEE

F

FRANCES LINCOLN
CHILDREN'S BOOKS

Contents

Here Come the Creatures...
One, Two, Three!

Here come the creatures,
　　one,
　　　　two,
　　　　　　three.
A crocodile's holding hands with a flea.
A tiger's arm-in-arm with a rat,
and a terrapin's toddling-on with a bat.
An elephant's side-by-side with a wren,
and a warthog's waddling along with a hen.
Here come the creatures,
　　eight,
　　　　nine,
　　　　　　ten.

8

Stroke the Cat

Stroke the cat,
stroke the cat,
and lift it from the floor.

Stroke the cat,
stroke the cat,
and shake hands with its paw.

Stroke the cat,
stroke the cat,
and scratch its head once more.

Stroke the cat,
stroke the cat,
and shoo it… through the door!

Garden Birds... Beware!

4 pigeons flutter down for bread.
6 seagulls glide high overhead.

5 sparrows peck at tiny crumbs.
1 robin in the winter comes.

3 swallows don't stay here too long.
2 blackbirds sing their evening song.

And... in the bushes... lying flat
there lurks **1** hungry ginger cat.

Watching a Bumble-Bee

Out in the garden you will see
the oh-so-busy bumble-bee.

It never stops to take a rest.
It wears an oh-so-hairy vest.

It gathers nectar all day long
and hums an oh-so-buzzy song.

While you watch from your garden seat
it's making honey oh-so-sweet,

then off it zigzags in a tizz
with oh-so-busy buzzy whizzzzzzzzzzzzzzzzzzzzzzzzz
zzzzzzzzzzzzzzzzzzzzzzzzzzzzzzzzzzzzzzzzzzzzzzzzzzz

Kiss Chase

Let's play Kiss Chase
in the garden
and run round the apple tree.
If you catch me
when I'm running
  then
      you
        kiss
          me!

Let's play Kiss Chase
at the seaside
down beside the water blue.
If I catch you
when you're running
    then
      I
        kiss
          you!

Roly Poly

Roly Poly,
roly poly,
down a grassy hill.
Roly poly,
roly poly,
just like Jack and Jill.

Roly poly,
roly poly,
on a sunny day.
Roly poly,
Roly poly,
what a game to play.

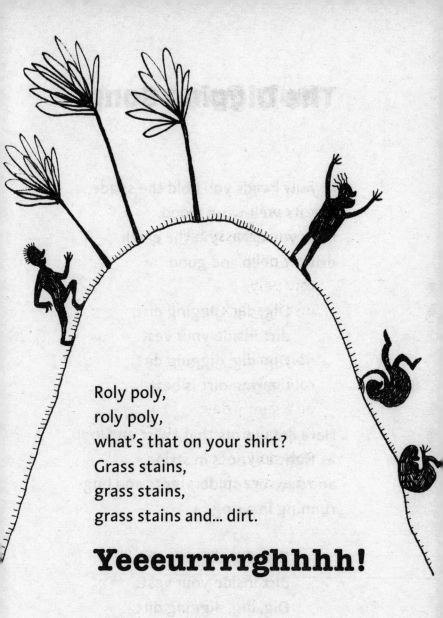

Roly poly,
roly poly,
what's that on your shirt?
Grass stains,
grass stains,
grass stains and... dirt.

Yeeeurrrrghhhh!

The Digging Song

In your hands you hold the spade,
feel its well-worn wood.
Now you drive it in the earth,
drive it deep and good.

> Dig, dig, digging dirt,
> dirt inside your vest.
> Dig, dig, digging dirt,
> digging dirt is best.

Here are worms that twist and loop,
as tight as knots in string,
and here are spiders, ants and bugs
running in a ring.

> Dig, dig, digging dirt,
> dirt inside your vest.
> Dig, dig, digging dirt,
> digging dirt is best.

Soon your hands are red and raw,
blisters on the way,
but your spade just wants to dig
all the long hot day.

Dig, dig, digging dirt,
dirt inside your vest.
Dig, dig, digging dirt,
digging dirt is best.

Summer Sun

Yes,
the sun shines bright
in the summer,
and the breeze
is soft
as a sigh.

Yes,
the days are long
in the summer,
and the sun
is king
of the sky.

The Red Boat

There goes the sun
slowly sailing by,
like a red boat
on the ocean of the sky.

There goes the sun
all the day through,
a red boat sailing
across its sea of blue.

Seaside Day

We're on our way this morning
for a day beside the sea,
there's Mum, there's Dad, there's little Gran
and my best friends
and me.
Seagulls glide far overhead
and the sun shines in the sky.
I unfold my yellow kite
and soon it's flying high.

> Hey,
> watch us race
> along the sand,
> running,
> running
> hand in hand.

We build a huge sandcastle
but it takes us half a day,
and then the tide comes rushing in
and washes it away.
We climb the highest sand dune,
then roll down without stop.
We end up in a laughing heap
. . . and climb back to the top.
     Hey,
     watch us race
     along the sand,
     running,
     running
     hand in hand.

With seaweed hung around our necks
we paddle in a pool.
Ice-cream cones and ice-cold drinks
all help to keep us cool.
Now it's late. The sun sinks down.
What a day beside the sea
for Mum, for Dad, for little Gran,
and my best friends
and me.

> Hey,
> how we raced
> along the sand,
> running,
> running
> hand in hand.

Going to Gran's

The car is packed,
we're on our way.
We're off to Gran's
on holiday.
We pass my school,
the park, the shop.
At traffic lights
we have to stop.
We travel on,
we leave the town,
now fields are green
and hills are brown.
We pass a farm,
I see some sheep,
a horse, a goat...
I fall asleep.

"We're here!" Mum calls.
"You've slept all day!"
I open eyes.
There's Gran! Hooray!
Away from town
we've come to stay
at my old Gran's
on holiday.

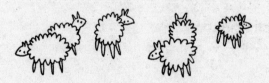

Happy Eid!

"*Happy Eid!*" we shout to all
as we run down the street.

We're on our way to Grandma's house
where friends and family meet.

We're all dressed in our very best
for this most special day.

At Gran's we'll give our gifts with love,
and "*Happy Eid!*" we'll say.

A Card for my Dad

This is the card I've made for my dad.
It's sticky with glue, but it's not too bad.

I've cut out a ship and I've stuck it in,
and I've drawn a shark with a great big fin.

Then I've written as neatly as I can,
"With love to my dad, the world's best man!"

This is the card I'll give to my dad.
It's sticky with glue, but it's not too bad.

Sam's Staying with Me

Sam is one of my friends.
Today he's feeling sad.
His mum has gone to hospital,
and Sam has got no dad.

My mum's invited Sam
to stay here at our house.
He looks upset and tearful,
and he's quiet as a mouse.

We've had fried egg and chips,
and now we'll watch TV.
While his mum's in hospital
Sam's staying with me.

Amy and her Harp

Amy calls
   her harp
      'The Tree of Strings',

     and when
   she plays
it sings, it sings!

Drink a Glass of Lemonade

Drink a glass of lemonade.
    Gurgle,
    gurgle,
    glug.

Second glass of lemonade.
    Gurgle,
    gurgle,
    glug.

Third glass of lemonade.
Now you'd better stop.
One more glass of lemonade
   and
   you'll
   go

POP!

Bounce-a-Ball

With my friends at playtime
  I play bounce-a-ball.
    It's bounce-a-ball to Emma
      and it's bounce-a-ball to Paul,
       it's bounce-a-ball to Ahmed
         and it's bounce-a-ball to Faz,
          it's bounce-a-ball to Guljit
            and it's bounce-a-ball to Baz,
           it's bounce-a-ball to Stacey
             and it's bounce-a-ball to Matt,
            it's bounce-a-ball to Sophie
          and it's bounce-a-ball to Pat,
         it's bounce-a-ball to Jeeta
       and it's bounce-a-ball to Luke,
      it's bounce-a-ball to Hanna
     and it's bounce-a-ball to Duke,
       it's bounce-a-ball to Chloe

and it's bounce-a-ball to Wayne,
it's bounce-a-ball to Amy
and it's bounce-a-ball to Shane.
There goes the school bell.
Now our playtime ends.
I played bounce-a-ball
with
my
best
friends.
Hey!

Who Likes Pancakes?

"Who likes pancakes?
Who likes beans?
Who likes pizza?
Who likes greens?
Who likes apples?
Who likes cheese?
Who likes pudding?
Who likes peas?
Who likes ice-cream
for their tea?
Mum
  and
    Dad
      and
        Gran
          and
            Me."

What's Yellow?

The full moon
on a cold winter's night.

A candle's flame,
all sparkly and bright.

Buttercups
in the field where you run.

And daffodils
that bloom in the sun.

But the yellow
I really like the most

is butter melting
on thick, warm toast.

Yummmmm!

When the Funfair Comes to Town

See the coloured lights that flash,
hear the dodgems when they crash,
give the coconuts a bash
    when the Funfair comes to town,
      when the Funfair comes to town.

Smell the burgers, peas and pies,
wear a mask with wobbly eyes,
throw a hoop and win a prize
      when the Funfair comes to town.
      when the Funfair comes to town.

See the crowds come in and out,
hear the children squeal and shout,
climb aboard the roundabout
when the Funfair comes to town,
when the Funfair comes to town.

Taste the toffee you can share,
hear loud music in the air,
ride the Ghost Train... if you dare
when the Funfair comes to town,
when the Funfair comes to town.

The Skipping Line

In skips Sarah,
    and in skips Sam.
    In skips Ahmed,
    and in skips Pam.
    In skips Precious,
    and in skips Dee.
    In skips Leroy,
    and then
    in skips
    me.

See how we skip,
all in a line.
Six skip, seven skip,
eight skip, nine.
Then on skip ten
we give a big shout
when the rope gets caught
and we
all fall
OUT!

Blowing Up a Big Red Balloon

You blow blow
blow blow blow
and the big red balloon
starts to
grow grow grow.

You puff puff
puff puff puff
until the big red balloon's
had enough
nuff nuff.

Just one more blow.

Oh no!

BANG!

Jamie Jefferson Jones

Up the stairs
and up the stairs
went Jamie Jefferson Jones.
He heard a creak,
he heard a squeak,
he heard some grumbling groans.
He heard a sigh,
he heard a cry,
he heard some mumbling moans
did Jamie Jefferson,
      Jamie Jefferson,
         Jamie Jefferson Jones.

Down the stairs
and down the stairs
ran Jamie Jefferson Jones.
"Mum, what a scare
I had up there!
I heard some ghostly groans!
I heard a wheeze,
I heard a sneeze,
I heard some rattling bones!"
cried Jamie Jefferson,
Jamie Jefferson,
Jamie Jefferson Jones.

Mum shook her head.
She laughed, and said,
"Jamie Jefferson Jones,
you silly man
that's only Gran
*on her **two** mobile phones!*
To bed upstairs
and no more scares,
and no more rattling bones,
my Jamie Jefferson,
> *Jamie Jefferson,*
> > *Jamie Jefferson Jones!"*

Odd Socks in the Morning

A spotty sock,
a spotty sock,
with half-a-dozen holes.

A silly sock,
a silly sock,
with orange mice and moles.

A soggy sock,
a soggy sock.
Oh, no! It's Baby Joe's!

A smelly sock,
a smelly sock.
It makes you hold your nose.

Dressing Up

Ben can be a Pirate,
and Faye can be a Clown.
Hal can be a Postman
walking round the town.

Jo can be a Princess,
and Mitch can be a Knight.
Fran can be a Monster
and give us all a fright.

Paul can be a Spaceman,
and Em can be the Queen.
Jack can be a Giant
dressed in red and green.

Jess can be a Cowgirl,
and George can be the King.
Jazz can be a Wizard
with a magic ring.

Matt can be a Doctor,
And Nik can be a Nurse.
And I will be the teacher
reading out this verse.

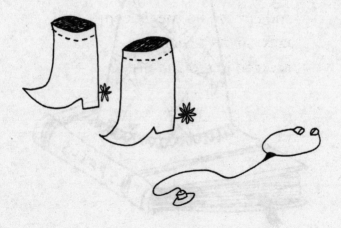

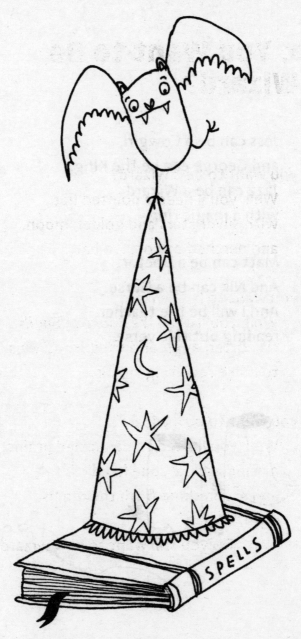

So, You Want to Be a Wizard?

So, you want to be a wizard?
    Well, you'll need a pointed hat
    with silver stars and golden moon,
    and perched on top. . . a bat.

So, you want to be a wizard?
    Well, you'll need '*Ye Booke of Spells*',
    six rotten eggs, and fried frogs' legs
    to make revolting smells.

So, you want to be a wizard?
    Well, you'll need some pickled brains,
    a wand, a cloak, one headless rat,
    and green slime from the drains.

        Do you *still* want to be a wizard?

My Teachers

My teacher's name
is Mrs Large.
She's helped
by Mrs Small.

Miss Thin comes in
and she pins up
our pictures
on the wall.

Big Mr Big's
the music man,
and he takes us
in the Hall.

There are
so *many* teachers
and I really like
them all.

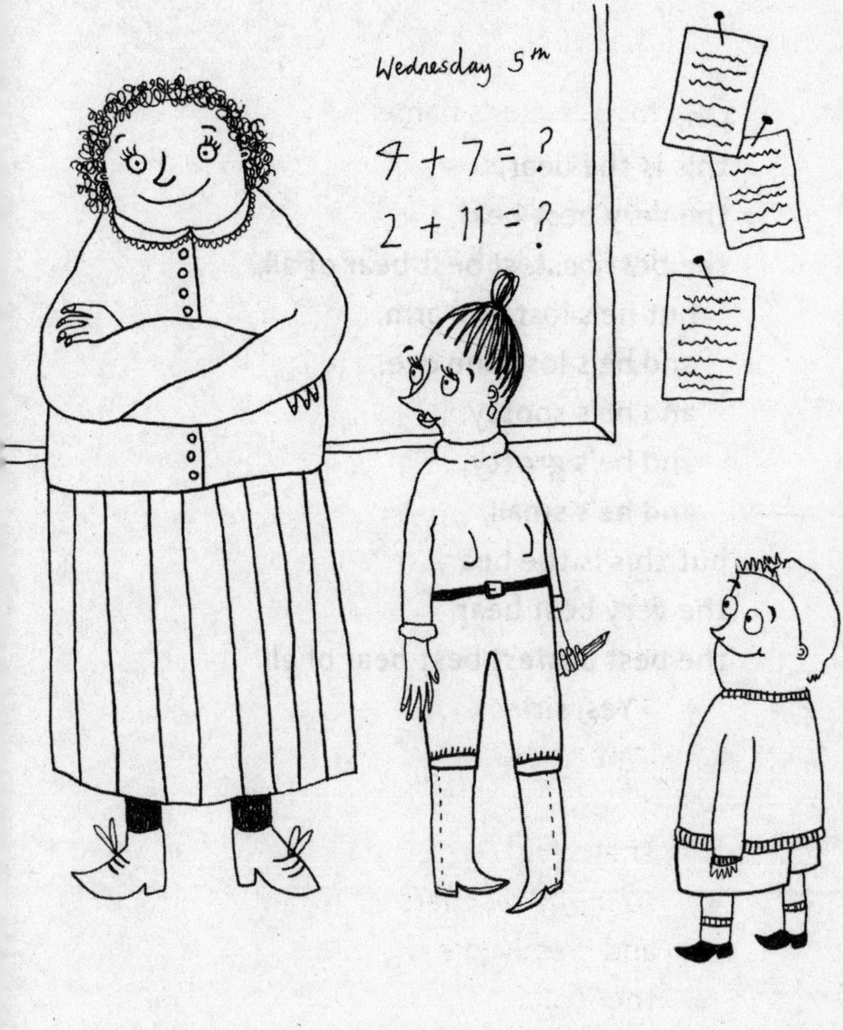
Wednesday 5th
4 + 7 = ?
2 + 11 = ?

The Bestest Bear Song

Oh,
this is the bear,
the very best bear,
the best *bestest* best bear of all,
   but he's lost one arm,
   and he's lost one eye,
   and he's spotty,
   and he's grotty,
   and he's small,
but this is the bear,
the very best bear,
the best *bestest* best bear of all.
     Yes, sir!

Oh,
he's wobbly and worn,
and his left ear is torn,
but he's been with me
since the day I was born,
   and I love,
   oh I love
   his soft fur,
for this is the bear,
the very best bear,
the best *bestest* best bear of all.
      Yes, sir!

With Gran and Rusty at the Vet's

We sit and wait
  to see the Vet.
    We're here with Rusty,
      Gran's sick pet.

    She's a kitten
    Gran took in,
  a starving stray,
so weak and thin.

Gran found Rusty
  at her back door,
    with bitten ear
      and poorly paw.

In her basket
Rusty cries
and looks at us
with big round eyes.

We wait with Rusty,
Gran's sick pet,
we sit and wait
to see the Vet.

Gran's Old Diary

I found my gran's old diary,
it has a lock and key.
I found it in the attic,
when you explored with me.

My gran wrote her old diary
years and years ago.
She used the blackest ink
on pages white as snow.

And inside Gran's old diary
something caught my eye:
one tiny buttercup
pressed flat from years gone by.

I'll never lose Gran's diary
or its silver key
that we found in the attic
when you explored with me.

Painting Pictures

It's fun to brush on pinks and reds
 and watch the colours run.
I love to splash on yellow blobs.
  What is it?
   It's the sun!

It's fun to splosh the orange on
 and lots of green and blue.
And now I'll add some purple spots.
  Who is it?
   You!
    It's you!

In Bluebell Wood

A million leaves
on trees so tall.
You'll hear birds sing
and cuckoos call
   in Bluebell Wood.

See butterflies,
hear pigeons coo.
The long grass is
still wet with dew
   in Bluebell Wood.

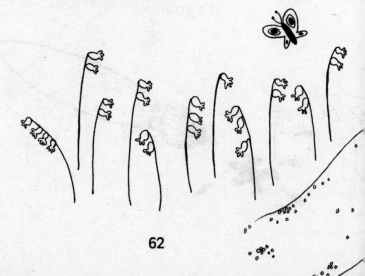

Look! Ferns unfurl,
and green frogs leap.
Brown rabbits hop
and beetles creep
    in Bluebell Wood.

A stile to climb.
A sunny day.
Just stand and watch
the bluebells sway
    in Bluebell Wood.

Mad March Hare

He runs so fast
  with ears a-flopping.
    There he goes,
      and he's not stopping!

Zooooooooooooooom!

The Music of the Wind

The wind
makes **LOUD** music.
It roars above the rooftops,
it drums beneath the floor,
it howls around the gable-end
and rat-a-tats the door.

The wind
makes quiet music.
It whistles down the chimney,
it tiptoes through a tree,
it hums against the window-pane,
and whispers tunes to me.

The Autumn Leaves

In autumn
the trees wave in the wind
and the leaves come tumbling
    down,
        down,
            down,
                down.

Here they come,
hundreds and thousands of leaves
in yellow, red,
    hazel,
        gold
           and
                chocolate brown.

Seagulls

The seagulls glide
above the town.
We throw out scraps
and they swoop down.
One seagull,
two seagulls,
three seagulls,
four!
With a shriek
and a squawk
here come

more,

more,

more!

Diwali! Diwali!

Diwali! Diwali!
Light the lamps
right now!

Let the flames so small and bright
guide us through the darkest night.
Let the flames so small and bright
lead us safely to the light.

Diwali! Diwali!
Light the lamps
right now!

One Day?

One day
we'll land on planet Mars.

One day
we'll travel to the stars.

One day
we'll live upon the moon.

This year?

Next year?

One day?

Soon?

Coal Fire in December

It's just great,
in icy December,
to get home
and chuck off
coat, gloves,
boots, scarf
   and hat,

and, *ahhhhhhhh*,
sit in front
of a glowing coal fire
and hear the warmth
purrrrrrrrrrring
like a contented
   cat.

The Sweeper in the Snowy Street

Snow fell silently in the night
  and now the street is frosty white.

I watch a man with snowy feet
  go slowly sweeping down the street.

His heavy boots have ice-capped toes.
  An icicle hangs from his nose.

With snow-topped hat he seems so old,
  this lonely figure in the cold.

Along the street I watch him go,
  a snowman sweeping in the snow.

Calling, Calling

The sky is grey,
and flakes are falling.
I hear the snowmen
calling, calling.

Outside it's wild.
Dad's car is st-st-stalling.
Next door my friends are
calling, calling.

Sliding, sledging,
and, yes, snowballing!
The winter winds are
calling, calling.

Santa's Sleigh

There it goes
where snowflakes fly!
Can you see it
in the sky?

Fast over sand dunes,
fast over seas,
fast over towers
and tunnels and trees.
Fast over highlands,
fast over hills,
fast over marshes
and meadows and mills.
Fast over forests,
fast over farms,
fast over bridges
and badgers and barns.

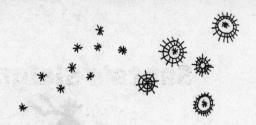

Fast over dovecotes,
fast over downs,
fast over taverns
and tide-ways and towns.

There it goes
where snowflakes fly!
Can you see it
in the sky?

75

Fast over castles,
fast over camps,
fast over roadworks
and railways and ramps.
Fast over harbours,
fast over homes,
fast over geysers
and gardens and gnomes.
Fast over shipwrecks,
fast over streets,
fast over funfairs
and frog-ponds and fleets.
Fast over landfills,
fast over lanes,
fast over districts
and ditches and drains.

There it goes
where snowflakes fly!
Did you see it
In the sky?

Questions on Christmas Eve

But... how can his reindeer fly without wings?
    Jets on their hooves? That's plain cheating!
And... how can he climb down the chimney pot
    when we've got central heating?

You say it's all magic and I shouldn't ask
    about Santa on Christmas Eve.
But I'm confused by the stories I've heard.
    I don't know what to believe.

I said that I'd sit up in bed all night long
    to see if he really would call.
But I fell fast asleep, woke up after dawn
    as something banged in the hall.

I saw my sock crammed with apples and sweets:
    there were parcels piled high near the door.
Jingle bells tinkled far off in the dark.
    One snowflake shone on the floor.

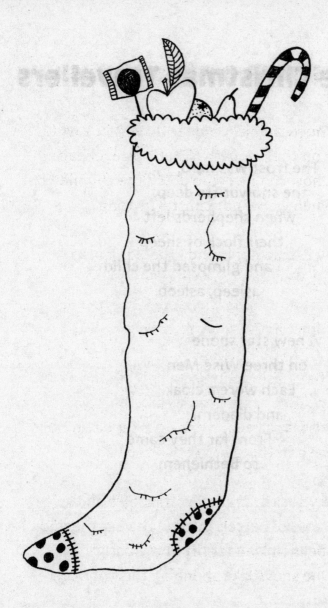

The Christmas Travellers

The frost was hard,
the snowdrifts deep,
when shepherds left
their flock of sheep
and glimpsed the child
asleep, asleep.

A new star shone
on three Wise Men.
Each wore a cloak
and diadem.
From far they came
to Bethlehem.

Books at Bedtime

Here a wizard casts a spell.
Here big giants roar and yell.
Here are rabbits having fun.
Here's an island in the sun.
Here the tortoise wins the race.
Here's a rocket lost in space.
Here are children on a beach.
Here's a magic flying peach.
Here green monsters come and go.
Here's old Santa in the snow.
Here's the wolf at Grandma's door.
    Eleven
      books
        (*yawn!*)
     piled
       on
      the
    floor.

Above Our Town

Above the houses
stars so bright
are twinkling twinkling
in the night.

Above the rooftops
of our town
a sad-faced moon
is gazing down.

In Creepy Castle

In Creepy Castle
ghosts in grey
are crying, flying
through the day.
        Woooooooooo!

In Creepy Castle
ghosts in white
are groaning, moaning
through the night.
        Oooooooooooh!

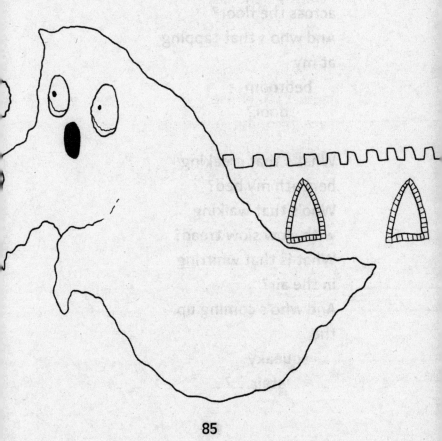

What's that....?

What's that scratching
at the window-pane?
Who's that knocking
again and again?
What's that creeping
across the floor?
And who's that tapping
at my
    bedroom
       door?

What's that creaking
beneath my bed?
Who's that walking
with slow slow tread?
What is that whirring
in the air?
And who's coming up
the
    squeaky
       stair...?

I lie in bed
and I'm wide awake.
The noises make me
shiver and shake.
But soon all's quiet
and the dark is deep
so I close my eyes
and...
        fall...
                asleep....

Counting Sheep

They said,
*"If you can't get to sleep
try counting sheep."*
I tried.
It didn't work.

They said,
*"Still awake? Count rabbits, dogs,
or leaping frogs."*
I tried.
It didn't work.

They said,
"It's very late. Count rats
or vampire bats!"
I tried.
It didn't work.

They said,
"Stop counting stupid sheep!
Eyes closed! Don't peep!"
I tried,

and fell asleep.

WES MAGEE is a former primary school teacher
and head teacher who resigned to become
a full-time author in 1990. He has published more
than 100 books for children – stories, plays, poetry,
anthologies, picture books, and information books.
His book of poems, *The Very Best of Wes Magee*,
won the Children's Poetry Bookshelf Award.

Wes regularly presents his 'Poetry and Book Show'
in schools around the world, and also runs
writing workshops. He lives in Potter Brompton,
a tiny hamlet on the Yorkshire Wolds,
where he has a dog (a Golden Retriever called Maya)
and a shoal of goldfish.
www.wesmagee.com

978-1-84780-168-5 • PB • £5.99

Perfect for younger children, these poems are
fresh, funny and brilliant for reading aloud.

"These poems are born out of years of
visiting infant classrooms.
A real birthday party of words" –
Pie Corbett

978-1-84780-340-5 • PB • £5.99

Poems about me, about you, about everyone in the class. Poems about friendship, playing games, teachers, bullying, jealousy, quarrels and secrets… Funny, thoughtful and entertaining, Cheryl Moskowitz's debut collection is right in tune with what goes on inside and outside the classroom.

"Look inside this book and see
a variety show: verses with instructions,
explanations, wisdoms and trousers that grow."
John Hegley

978-1-84780-341-2 • PB • £5.99

Meet sensational scorers, dependable defenders,
great goalkeepers and fanatical fans
like Great Gran. Find out who always shouts
at the ref, what is scary about being in the wall
and why you shouldn't put Mum in goal.
Every aspect of the football season and more
are brilliantly brought to life by poet and
football fan Paul Cookson, Poet-in-Residence
at the National Football Museum.

"Dazzling football poetry." – *BBC Sport*

978-1-84780-169-2 • PB • £5.99

From spooky legends to dreamy poems,
teasers and rhymes, expect the unexpected.
A poetry adventure waiting to happen!

"A poet with a powerful feeling for story
and language" – *Carousel*

978-1-84780-366-5 • PB • £6.99

Chickens who wear jumpers, all kinds
of monsters, a puppy's favourite chews
(a lucky dip of forgotten socks),
staying awake waiting for your birthday,
a bear in his underwear…. In his first
collection for younger children, well-known
poet Brian Moses has provided a funny
and witty snapshot of family life, with
a bit of fantasy added in. Perfect for
sharing at home or at school.